A BUTTERFLY'S TEETH

BY ALBERT LAMPO JR.

ILLUSTRATIONS BY PEGGY GRINVALSKY

enjoy our little book

Peggy Grinvalsky

Best wishes!

Albert Lampo Jr.

To Dad, Albert Sr., my hero and role model.
And to Chong who inspires me to take risks.

Albert Lampo Jr.

To Jhan, for his lively curiosity and care free love of life.
To Que-ena who tucks me into bed when I'm cranky.
And to my mother and father who surrounded me
with nature, books and music

Peggy Grinvalsky

I have a good friend whose name is Keith
And he wants to count a butterfly's teeth.
I asked my friend, "Why do such a chore?"
And he said, "Cause no one has done it before!"

"I can count her wings and I can count her feet.
I can count her colors so pretty and neat.
I can count her legs and her antennae
And I'll count her ears if she has any.

"I can count her wings and I can count her feet.
I can count her colors so pretty and neat.
I can count her legs and her antennae
And I'll count her ears if she has any.

I can count when she flies. I can count when she lands.
I can count when she sits. I can count when she stands.
I can count all of this and so could you
But counting her teeth is difficult to do!

Do you think she uses a tiny toothbrush,
When she can find the time, when she's not in a rush?
Does she gargle and rinse to make her teeth whiter?
Does she floss with a thread that's spun by a spider?

Is there a butterfly dentist that she can go to
When a toothache makes her unable to chew?
Do you think he makes tiny butterfly braces
to straighten the teeth in butterflies' faces?

If I could get a good look at her mug
I could count the teeth of this beautiful bug.
A peek in her mouth I'm hoping will show
Answers to questions I'm curious to know.

So this I asked of my little friend Keith,
"How will you see the butterfly's teeth?"

"I shall get very close, I think at first.
When the butterfly comes to quench her thirst
She'll stick out her tongue and roll back her lips.
Perhaps then I will see them, if only their tips.

So far I've failed though I've tried for a while."
I suggested, "Keith, make the butterfly smile."
Keith said, "Ok, maybe I will.
But first I must get one to simply sit still!

They flutter and fly all over the place.
It's hard to get a look at a butterfly's face!
I said, "Hold a flower outstretched in your hand.
If you're patient and wait, maybe one will land."

Keith said, "I'm not sure how to get her to grin.
Should I tickle her belly? Should I tickle her chin?
Should I use my finger to give her a poke?
Should I get close to her ear and tell her a joke?

I've tried to catch her but she flies off in alarm
And holding her, I thought, might cause her harm.
So I must try some other way
If it takes an hour or it takes all day.

If I ask her real nice and say pretty please
Do you think I could coax her until she says cheese?
If I lie on my back and look up from beneath
From there do you think I could count her teeth?"

"Keith, why not count birds or clouds or petals on flowers?
Or wait til tonight and count stars for hours?
Why not count ants or the leaves on trees,
Or the warts on a toad or the knees of bees?

You could count rocks or snails or sticks in the yard.
What you're trying to do just seems so hard!"
He said, "I counted those all through the Spring.
But a butterfly's teeth! That's such a special thing!"